The

MAFIA DON
of the
USA.

Samuel Manzano

Author's Tranquility Press
MARIETTA, GEORGIA

Samuel Manzano/Author's Tranquility Press
2706 Station Club Drive SW
Marietta, GA 30060
www.authorstranquilitypress.com

Publisher's Note: This is a work of fiction. Names, characters, places, and incidents are a product of the author's imagination. Locales and public names are sometimes used for atmospheric purposes. Any resemblance to actual people, living or dead, or to businesses, companies, events, institutions, or locales is completely coincidental.

Ordering Information:
Quantity sales. Special discounts are available on quantity purchases by corporations, associations, and others. For details, contact the "Special Sales Department" at the address above.

The Mafia Don of the USA/Samuel Manzano
Hardback: 978-1-959197-97-3
Paperback: 978-1-959197-98-0
eBook: 978-1-959197-99-7

CONTENTS

THE MAFIA DON OF THE USA. CAST

Tony Defeo..The New Don

Tony Banuchi.................................. Leader Of Young Turks

Nania Agostino................................Mother Of Tony Banuchi

Joe Pagano...Tony's Best Friend

Frank Orsini............................Worships Tony-Childhood Friend

Nancy Traves......................................Mother Of Joe Traves

Joe Traves...................................... FBI. Agent Task Force N.Y.C.

Bill Gonzalez...................New York City C0p Part Of Task Force

John Costello...................New York City Cop Part Of Task Force

Joe Fortuno...Mayor Of New York City

Joe Taousie............................. Deputy Mayor Of New York City

Frank Dágostino................Police Comisioner Of New York City

Spanish Rey...............................Crime Boss Of Spanish Harlem

Big Sam Small......................................Crime Boss Of Harlem

Joe Gomez...State Senator For New York

Mike Torsino.......................................Congressman For Brooklyn

Frank Brown ....Congressman For Manhatan

Jim Healey....................................Congressman For The Bronx

John Kelly..................................City Councilman For Manhattan

CHAPTER 1

There is a meeting of the commission of organize crime in the USA better known as the Mafia, the reason for this meeting is that the Don of the Mafia has been send to prison and a new leader must be chosen, but they have a big problem they cannot reach a vote on who should be the new Don because no one has the overall confidence of the commission to replace the old Don.

AFTER MANY HOURS OF DEBATE

TONY GRAZIANO from Chicago

It's a shame Tony is not alive because he would be perfect no doubt about him, there we would all agreed.

JOE PAGANO from New York City

He is not dead. I know where he is and I can contact him if you all agreed that is the man to replace the old man....... Everybody agreed he is the one.

TONY GRAZIANO

Call him where ever he is and ask him to comeback, we need him.

THEN EVERYONE STARTS TO ASK WHY DID HE DISAPPEAR

TONY GRAZIANO

Joe why did he disappear 25 years ago he was the number one men of the old Don, who was like a father with him.

JOE PAGANO

He had his reasons for leaving, he has been living in Puerto Rico in the west part of the island for the past 18 years he keeps to himself, I send him some money to start a small bar with good food he keeps low profile he is using a SS # of someone who is decease and no one will missed, that's why the feds have not located him besides with the beard and mustache he has even I when I saw him, I did not recognize him until he came to me and said hello, that was after I slip the feds after arriving in Puerto Rico.

TONY GRACIANO

Do you think he will go for it after some many years away and, why did he leave everything he had I mean give me one good reason when you were the heir and no one to oppose you?

JOE PAGANO

There was a reason and if I was you, I would not ask him.

MICKEY MIRANDA FROM CALIFORN

How do you think TONY BANUCHI is going to take this, these young TURKS think they can do what they want now that the DON is away.

SAMMY FROM DETROIT

They don't know Tony; they were kids when he left, BANUCHI was not even born yet.

JOE

We are the commission and have to back him up if he comes back, I will fly down tonight and see what he thinks maybe he doesn't know the old man is in jail. Everyone stay put until I get back on Sunday or with him or without him then we decide what we will do. At least I am sure a lot of the Politicians in New York Will remember who he is.

CHAPTER 2

PUERTO RICO

JOE

He arrives in Puerto Rico, he checks in at his hotel, and takes a cab to RIO PIEDRAS PUBLIC MARKET, there he mingles with the people.

There is an employee of Tony waiting for him on one of the side streets of Capetillo ....

There he is pickup and heads to RINCON; he arrives at TONYS bar.

TONY

I have not been so happy to see anyone in a long time like I am today, tell me, how is everybody especially the old man.

JOE

TONY, don't you know the old man was sent to prison for 40 years?

TONY SHOUTS

WHEN THE HELL THAT HAPPENED, I DON'T KNOW A FUCKING THING ABOUT THAT! Why didn't you call me, you of all people know what he means to me, he was the father I never met.

JOE

Tony, we have a big problem back home, and you are the only solution to the problem. The commission cannot get together about the new DON. The only person where everyone agreed ...is with you as the new DON, and we also have a problem with the Young Turk's, since the old man was sent away, they think they can take over, there is no respect and the police are on our back and the Politian's are not cooperating with us.

Tony, we need you, forget what happen that was an accident only you and me know what happen the old man is in jail, he will never know unless you tell him. But IF you love the old man, come back and take over, even in prison he would be happy knowing that your back and took over for him.

TONY

What does the rest of the commission think?

JOE

Everyone agreed that if you came back, we would all back you.

TONY

Starts thinking about the old man and how close they were he walks toward the beach and comes back.

JOE

Except we have a problem, we have a Young Turk Who thinks since the old man was sent away, he can do whatever he wants; he is the leader of all the others.

TONY

Who is his father?

JOE

Michael BANUCHI. He was killed 5 years ago; his mother is NANIA AGOSTINO, you remember her? You were sweet on her until you broke off with her, well after that she married BANUCHI.

TONY

Yes, I remember her. She was part of the reason I left New York City.

JOE

You never mentioned her as part of the reason I always thought it was about the accident.

TONY

I will return. I owe it to the old man. Let me set everything down here and we will have the meeting on Friday the 13 and no phones. We will get together at GINOS Place at MULBERRY remember no talking on the phones about the meeting, by the way, I want this young BANUCHI to be present—you make sure he is there. You call me Thursday on a safe phone, I will let you know what flight and time that I will arrive on Thursday and I will let you know how we are going to handle the meeting.

JOE

I assure you, young Tony will be there.

TONY

Do not forget, no phones otherwise, we will have a party for the feds and the New York cops. I want to see their faces when they find out I'm back. I have not done anything except I just disappear for the last 22 years, that's no crime. Get back to New York and call me THURSDAY MORNING—JOE CALLS TONY Tony what time and flight are you on, I have an apartment for you for the time being until we set you up in a permanent place.

TONY

I arrive at 7:30 P.M. on flight 310, I have no luggage so I will be buying new clothes on Friday. I will need you all day Friday so make your arrangements for Friday and who knows until when by the way with all the business about the old man, I never ask you how is your wife and my godchild, whom I have never seen and what is he doing.

JOE

My wife is fine and she is dying to see you, your godchild is a teacher at New York University and he has a picture of you in his room, so he has known who his Godfather is all his life. See you tonight, Don Tony. Take care of yourself J F K AIRPORT.

JOE

Welcome home Tony, the first thing we are going to do is go to the best Italian restaurant in little Italy and ORSINI is waiting for us, we three have not been together for many years and later, we talk about business and anything else on your mine but tonight, I am the DON understood any questions that's what you always say so there is no misunderstanding, so let us enjoy ourselves.

TONY

Joe, I must say I agreed with you, so let's go where ever it is and enjoy my returning home and tomorrow, we start to work but tonight, it's for us three after so many years.

JOE

Since you do not have any luggage, let us get the hell out of here. MOTT STREET –LOMBARDIS RESTAURANT.

ORSINI

Tony, I cannot believe it is you. After so many years, tonight, we celebrate us three together after so many years.

JOE

Let us make a toast first to our friendship and then to the new DON of the USA. THEY CELEBRATE ALL NIGHT.

CHAPTER 3

MEETING AT GINOS PLACE

BANUCHI

Hey ORSINI, what's all the mystery about this get together what am I going to be part of the commission because everyone here is from the commission, come on let me in on the big surprise.

ORSINI

Don't you worry kid, you will find out soon enough. Enjoy yourself and SHUTUP.

JOE COMES OUT OF THE BACK ROOM, HE WISPER'S TO ORSINI TO LOWER THE DRAPE'S AND FOR EVERYONE TO MOVE TO THE BACK ROOM, ONE BY ONE THERE GOING TO MOVE TO ANOTHER PLACE, KEEP SHUT THE PLACE COULD BE BUG BY THE FEDS TONY HAD PICK THIS PLACE BECAUSE IT HAD A SECRET TUNNAL, THE OLD MAN HAD SHOWING HIM WHEN HE WAS YOUNG IT COME'S OUT 3 BUILDING'S AWAY, IT WAS FROM THE

OLD TIMES WHEN THE OLD DON WAS YOUNG AND WAS IN BOOTLEGGING.

(THE MEETING BEGINS)

AS ALL OF THE MEN START ARRIVING, EVERYONE IS HAPPY TO SEE TONY AGAIN AND AFTER ALL OF THE HELLO'S TONY.

JOE, you begin the meeting and start with the agreement that they made with you, I will take it from there.

JOE SPEAKS LOUD

LET' S ALL GET DOWN TO WHAT WE ARE HERE FOR. TONY IS HERE JUST LIKE I TOLD YOU HE WOULD BE. HE DID NOT KNOW ABOUT THE OLD MAN GOING TO JAIL BUT HE IS BACK. HE OWES IT TO THE OLD MAN HE KNOW'S ABOUT THE PROBLEMS, AND THAT WE AGREED, HE WAS TOO OCCUPIED THE DONS CHAIR.

.... EVERYONE IS SILENT.

BANUCHI

So that's the Tony I have heard so much about. I thought he was dead and why is he back?

ORSINI

Kid, keep your mouth shut. If you want to leave this place alive, listen to what is going to happen and shut the fuck up.

TONY

You are all wondering why I left. That I will not explain, that's not any concern of anyone of you, is that understood? Do we all agree? Does anyone disagree? Any questions?

THERE IS SILENCE

THEN EVERYONE ANSWERS ITS O.K. WITH US

BANUCHI

I want to know why you are replacing the DON, and why was I invited to this meeting.

TONY

First, no one replaces the DON. I will sit in the chair but not replace him. Second, you are here because I ask for you to be present. I will get to you when I finish other matters. Understood MR. BANUCHI? Any questions?

BANUCHI

DOES NOT ANSWER, JUST NODS HIS HEAD AS A YES AND SITS DOWN.

ORSINI

I told you to keep your mouth shut. Do we understand each other?

BANUCHI

All right let's see what MR. DEFEO has to say to me.

TONY

The first thing I want is everything that we have on every politician in your states and in New York City, every bribe that the police have taken.

JOE, you take care of that and get back to me. That also is your job in New York. The second thing is a meeting with the five families in New York City. ORSINI, you will set that. The meeting will be outside the city. You pick the place that will be in one week. The rest of you will pick someone in your cities— BOSTON, CHICAGO, NEW ORLEANS, AND SAN FRANCISCO, to do the same. JOE and ORSINI will take care of New York City. I want that information in one week, any questions?

NO ONE ANSWER'S

When you are set, you will contact JOE. We will let you know how you will contact him and for your information, we are going legal believe it or not. I DON'T WANT ANYONE TO FUCK UP. AND LET THE FEDS KNOW SOMETHING IS GOING ON. ANY QUESTIONS?

NO ONE ANSWERS.

TONY

Now, I need to know how we are financially, so I know with what I can count. Now give me a break down of what is happening here, Joe. Let's start with you.

JOE

The police are hitting our gambling in the city, the same with the numbers and the YOUNG TURKS are wild with no respect since the old man was sent away, and the Jamaicans, Columbians and the Russians are a big problem.

TONY

That brings me to you ...MR. BANUCHI. I hear you are the leader of these boys who think they can do anything they want without answering to anyone now that the old man is not here. I understand the old man let you do many things without saying nothing about it.

He must have like you a lot because that was not normal with him; he loves discipline. So, you think about that, he is not here now—I am... and discipline is the rule with me. I learn it from him. The first mistake, I will consider. The second, I do not forgive. Do we understand each other?

TONY BANUCHI

Yes, I understand Tony.

TONY

I did not hear well. What did you say?

BANUCHI

I am sorry, Don TONY. It will not happen again.

TONY

By the way, who are your parents?

BANUCHI

My father was Michael BANUCHI and my mother is NANIA AGOSTINO.

TONY

A STRANGE LOOK COMES TO HIS FACE WHEN HE HEARS HER NAME.

TONY

I will be getting back to you, MR. BANUCHI about another matter I want to discuss with you, but that can wait. Give my regards to your mother.

We will all be getting together so I can see some of my old friends. Tell your mother I would like to see her there.

Well, you all know what you have to do, so let's get to work.

THE MEETING COMES TO AN END.

CHAPTER 4

THE HOME OF TONY BANUCHI

BANUCHI

HI MOM, how is everything? By the way, an old friend sends you regards.

NANIA

An old friend of mine who could that be?

BANUCHI

It's the new Don, TONY DEFEO?

NANIA

It cannot be. He is dead. That's what they have always said.

BANUCHI

Well, he looks pretty well for a dead man. Did you know him well mom? Who was he to the old DON?

NANIA

HE was like a son to him, but he disappeared one day and no one ever hear about him again until now.

BANUCHI

JOE PAGANO knew where he was because he contacted HIM and brought him back.

NANIA

SHE DOES NOT ANSWER AND ASKS HERSELF WHY DIDN'T JOE TELL HER TONY WAS ALIVE ALL THESE YEARS. THE MAN SHE HAS ALWAYS LOVED AND WHY DID HE COME BACK NOW.

BANUCHI

Well, you will see him soon. There is going to be a get-together to see his old friends.

NANIA

TONY, you have Joe's phone number. I need to speak with him.

BANUCHI

What do you need to talk to JOE about, MOM?

NANIA

Well, if he knew where TONY was, maybe he knows where ANNA IGLESIAS is. She was a close friend of us and I lost contact with her a long time ago.

BANUCHI

Sure Mom, his number is 765-4795. That's his private number. Don't give it to no one.

NANIA CALLS JOE

Hello JOE, its NANIA BANUCHI. I need to see you, it's very important and I cannot speak about it on the phone.

JOE

It's nice hearing from you, but what do you need to see me about?

NANIA

I cannot say it over the phone. Can you meet me at Washington square in about 30 minutes?

IT'S VERY IMPORTANT (SHE IS CRYING).

JOE

Take it easy. I will be there and calm down. Whatever your problem is, I will take care of it.

NANIA

Thank you! I'll see you there good bye.

CHAPTER 5

WASHINGTON SQUARE

NANIA

SHE ARRIVES AND SITS DOWN ON ONE OF THE BENCHES TO WAIT FOR JOE.

JOE

HE ARRIVES IN HIS CAR WITH ORSINI. LEAVES HIM IN THE CAR AND WALKS TOWARD NANIA.

JOE

NANIA, it's real nice to see you after so long.

NANIA shouts

CUT THE BULL SHIT, AND TELL ME WHY YOU NEVER TOLD ME THAT TONY WAS ALIVE, AND YOU KNEW WHERE YOU COULD CONTACT HIM, SO DON'T BS ME.

JOE

NANIA, I didn't know he meant so much to you, and I made a promise to TONY that I would not tell anyone where he was. And don't forget we lost touch and, I did not know you wanted to know about him...and do not forget you married BANUCHI, so how was I to know. Anyway, I cannot tell you anything about TONY, only he can tell you.

NANIA

JOE, I want to talk to him.

JOE

NANIA, TONY wants a get-together with the old crowd and you will see him. Don't ask anything because I cannot say a word.

I will let your son know. He will tell you where it's going to be.

NANIA

Give me his phone number, I will call him.

JOE

I cannot do that, there are too many things going on right now, and he cannot talk to you.

NANIA

Call him and tell him I am here that's all I ask.

JOE

Hello TONY, listen I have NANIA with me and she wants to speak to you.

TONY

Put her on.

NANIA, how are you? It's nice to hear you after so many years.

NANIA

Why didn't you let me know you were alive all these years?

TONY

NANIA, I cannot speak to you right now, give JOE your phone number, and I will call you.

HANGS UP

TONY

STARTS THINKING ABOUT HER WHEN THEY WERE YOUNG AND wanted to marry her, PHONE RINGS AND HE ANSWERS.

ORSINI

I have set up a meeting with the five families to discuss about New York.

TONY

Call me later and give me the details.

CHAPTER 6

CITY HALL MEETING

JOE TAOUSIE –DEPUTY MAYOR

MR. MAYOR, everything is alright since the old DON was sent to prison. Everything in the city has changed.

MAYOR JOE FORTUNO

Well, I don't like it because it's too quiet. No one has made a move to take his place. It's not normal for no one to try and take his place, something is happening and we don't know about it.

JOE TRAVES FBI

MR. MAYOR, times have changed. We have checked each of the five Bosses of the families very well, and none of them have the respect to lead, and they have another problem: Young BANUCHI. He only respected The Old DON and he has the young hot heads behind him, and they want to take over now. What could happen is an open war between BANUCHI and the old guard.

MAYOR

I still don't like it, something is happening and we do not know anything of what is going on.

JOE TRAVES

MR. MAYOR, it's all over. The DON is in jail and it will take a long time for them to get organized and come up with a New Don that all of them will respect and obey.

MAYOR

I'll tell you one thing if the DON'S right-hand man were alive, it would be a different ball game. That TONY was something else.

JOE TRAVES

Who was this TONY? Who was he?

MAYOR

I used to work in CITY HALL, the DON was one of the family Bosses and TONY was like a son to him. Don't know what happened to him. I guess they killed him because he just disappeared from the face of the earth.

JOE

I'll checkup on him and find out what happened to him. What's his name?

MAYOR

TONY DEFEO that was back in 1985 give it or take a year.

JOE

I'LL let you know what I find out and get back to you. Don't worry so much. I will be getting back to the office.

EVERYONE GETS UP AND WALKS OUT OF THE OFFICE

CHAPTER 7

HOME OF JOE TRAVEAS

JOE

HI MOM, how was your day today?

NANCY

How did it go with you today?

JOE

It went well, but now that the Don is in jail, they are afraid because they say it is too quiet and that something is going on. I try to convince them that none of the five heads of the New York families have the brains nor the respect to become the new Don of organized crime in the country. He always comes from one of the New York families, it has always been that way. It is like a tradition.

NANCY

Well, as long as it's like you say, I will be happy.

JOE

The Mayor is so afraid that he thinks that a guy who disappeared over 20 years ago might come back from the dead.

NANCY

And who could that be? Who disappeared so many years ago?

JOE

A guy who used to be like a son to the old DON. His name is TONY DEFEO. I'm going to check on him. HE must be dead because he just vanished, according to the Mayor.

NANCY

(IN HER MINE) ...SHE HAD NOT HEARD THAT NAME IN OVER...27 YEARS, her mind goes back to her youth and her first love, TONY DEFEO...she changes the conversation. Well, let's forget about this mystery man and see what you want for dinner.

JOE

Whatever you want, mom.

NANCY

Well, let us see what I get ready real fast for my boy.

CHAPTER 8

MEETING OF THE FIVE FAMILY'S HEADS

1 — TEDDY DECORSA   3 — TONY CAPELI

2 — RUDY GRACIANO   4 — JOHNNY GALLO

5 — FRANK LOMBARDY

JOE

Well, you all know why we are here. Let's see what tony has in mind for us in New York.

TONY WALK'S IN

TONY

Nice to see all of you again. Just like the old days but without the old man. I need to know how we are financially in New York because if we ask for these people to get off our backs, we have to pay for it for a while until we get organized again and the money from the numbers and casinos start rolling in again.

RUDY, you have a transportation company, I need you to put me on your payroll as VP So, I have a legal salary and also an expense account. I don't want problems with IRS.

We have to buy out several of your competition, so in that way, we are going to control 80 percent of all the transportation of bananas that hit these ports. We are going legal.

Joe, I need someone who is an expert in electronics. I mean wiretapping, bugging, and surveillance. We need to be as good as the feds and the cops. We are going to find out everything about these politicians and cops that we are paying off just in case they get a little greedy. Now, whoever you pick has to be clean from head to toe. You will fill me in on whoever it is later.

Now, who is running Harlem and Spanish Harlem?

JOE

Harlem is run by BIG SAMMY. He took over when his father was killed, and in Spanish Harlem it is Spanish REY son. You remember Spanish Rey?

TONY

Yeah, I remember him and the old man; he was O.K. You set up the meeting as soon as possible. I want to get that out of the way. I want everything in place as soon as possible. Once New York is set up, we go to CHICAGO. After the Harlem meeting, I want to get together with young Banuchi as soon as possible and see if you can set both meeting on the same day.

JOE, how are the old man's casinos doing, and by the way, who is the MAYOR of New York now?

JOE

His name is Joe FORTUNO.

TONY

Any relation to Mike FORTUNO.

JOE

His Son.

TONY SPEAKS LOUD

IN OTHER WORDS, THE DON PAID FOR HIS COLLEGE EDUCATION. I WANT YOU TO CHECK OUT ALL OF THE CHILDREN OF THE POLITICIANS WHO WERE ON THE OLD MAN'S BRIBES AND FIND OUT WHERE THEY ARE. LET'S SEE IF WE HAVE MORE POLITICIANS IN OUR POCKETS THAN WE KNOW. WHO KNOWS WHAT WE WILL FIND OUT.

JOE

The cops have hit us real hard, but we have several of the casinos running.

TONY SPEAKS LOUD

JOE, WHY DID THE OLD MAN LET THIS KID BANUCHI GETAWAY WITH ALL YOU SAID?

JOE

Nobody knows, but he did things with this kid that I could not believe. I MEAN he really liked this kid.

Maybe he reminded the old man about his kid, but I don't know.

TONY

JOE, where is the get-together going to be at.

JOE

I was thinking, where do you think would be the best place, and let's do it Saturday night.

TONY

Let's do it at the old social club at MULBERRY ST, that place is connected to the old tunnel, that way I can come in from the tunnel instead of the front it's better that way, JUST IN CASE ANYTHING HAPPENS THAT WE ARE NOT EXPECTING. Don't forget, when all these cars start arriving, it's going to call the attention. Anyway, let's do it there. Don't forget, place the men in front just in case we get a surprise visit from the cops. That will give me time to get out of there. You will pick me up and leave me at GINOS place. I'll go through the old way, come out under the club, and come out through the tunnel.

CHAPTER 9

MEETING AT MULBERRY ST. SOCIAL CLUB

AS THE CARS START ARRIVING, THE PEOPLE START TALKING ABOUT SOMETHING BIG HAPPENING. THEY HAVE NOT SEEN SOME OF THESE FACES IN A LONG TIME AND MUCH LESS TOGETHER.

MICKEY CAPUTO

Hey, what's going on here? What are all these expensive cars doing in the neighborhood? Some big shot died.

SOMEONE ANSWERS

MICKEY, I DONT KNOW IF SOMEONE DIED, BUT FOR ALL THESE GUYS GETTING TOGETHER IT'S BIG.

MICKEY CAPUTO

Pulls out his cell phone and makes a call. Hello, SARGENT COSTELLO, I have a big tip for you it's worth a couple of twenties.

COSTELLO

What's so important that's worth a couple of twenties?

MICKEY

There's a big get-together of the mob at the social club. I MEAN BIG FACES I HAVE NOT SEEN AROUND HERE IN YEARS.

COSTELLO

Write down some of the license plates and call me back later. Wait until they get started and then call me.

INSIDE THE CLUB, EVERYONE STARTS TO SAY HELLO AND ASKS FOR TONY.

JOE

Everybody take your seats, and let's close the door and the shades.

NANIA

Joe where's tony?

JOE

Take it easy. He will be here soon. We are just making sure we do not get any surprise visits from the cops. By the way, where is your kid?

NANIA

He's over there talking to his friends. WHY?

JOE

Nothing special, just that TONY wanted him to be here with you.

ALRIGHT EVERYBODY ENJOY YOURSELVES. WE HAVE GOOD REASONS TO BE HAPPY.

TONY WALKS IN FROM A BACK ROOM

EVERYONE GETS UP AND GO TOWARDS HIM TO GREET HIM AND WELCOME HIM BACK.

TONY

STARTS TO SHAKE HANDS WITH A LOT OF PEOPLE HE HAS NOT SEEN FOR MANY YEARS, AND GRADUALLY COME'S TO THE TABLE WERE NANIA AND HER SON ARE SITTING.

NANIA, you have not changed a bit in fact, you're more beautiful than the last time I saw you it is really good to see you again by the way I would like to speak to you later on, before you leave tonight.

(HE LOOKS AT HER SON BUT DOES NOT SAY A WORD TO THE YOUNG BANUCHI AND WALKS AWAY)

(TONY MINGLES WITH THE PEOPLE AND DRIFTS AWAY)

TONY

AFTER ABOUT AN HOUR, TONY WALKS TOWARD NANIA AND ASKS HER TO DANCE WITH HIM.

AS THEY DANCE

NANIA

Where have you been all of these years? Everyone thought you were dead, and why did you disappear like that?

TONY

I cannot explain anything to you. It is not the place nor the time. Tonight I am finding out who is against me in New York, including your son. I have been told the old man let him get away with a lot of things. JOE tells me he could never understand why. I am going to have a talk with him after I get things settled, I will get in touch with you but give me time, I have a lot of things in my mind right now.

Anyway, the reason that I left was not because we broke up. Anyway, it looks like you had a happy marriage and he gave you a son to remember him. I am sorry that he is not my son, but things happen. No use crying over spilled milk just wish it had not happened.

NANIA

(Starts thinking this cannot be happening to me, tony against Tony. It cannot happen)

THEY WALK AWAY FROM EACH OTHER...NANIA STARTS TO LOOK FOR HER SON.

(Outside in the street)

MICKEY CAPUTO

SGT. COSTELLO, I have your plate numbers, but nobody knows what this party is all about.

SGT.COSTELLO

Give me the numbers you call me if something happens. I have to call the Captain, and let him know about this.

COSTELLO SPEAKS LOUD

CAPTAIN, I JUST GOT A TIP. THERE'S A BIG MAFIA PARTY AT THE MULBERRY ST. SOCIAL CLUB —A LOT OF BIG FACES. WHAT DO YOU WANT ME TO DO?

CAPTAIN

They are probably trying to find the new Don in a whisky bottle. They are like little boys who just lost their father and don't know what to do. Forget it, and go about your work.

(INSIDE THE CLUB)

TONY

JOE, I want to talk to BANUCHI tonight and get that out of the way, and do not forget, call Big Sam and Spanish Rey.

JOE

I will tell BANUCHI to stay, that you want to talk to him.

JOE

 Walks toward the table were NANIA and her Son Are.

BANUCHI, TONY WANTS TO TALK TO YOU, SO STAY AFTER EVERYONE LEAVES.

NANIA

He has to take me home. Tell tony to see him later.

JOE

No problem. ORSINI will take you home, NANIA.

NANIA

Joe where is Tony? I don't see him.

JOE

He is over there at the bar.

NANIA WALKS AWAY TOWARDS THE BAR

NANIA

TONY, I need to speak to you about something.

TONY

Sure, is something wrong? You look nervous.

NANIA WITH A FIRM VOICE

WHAT DO YOU WANT WITH MY SON?

TONY

NANIA I just want to speak with him and since we are all here, I decided to speak to him tonight. But don't you worry about him, I just want to get a couple of things straight with him, but if it's going to upset you, then I do not want to do. After so many years without seeing you, I'll see him later. You go home with your son, O.K.? Now give me a big smile and enjoy yourself, and don't worry, nothing will happen to him. You're the last person I would hurt in the world.

NANIA

Thank you, Tony. Don't forget to call me later.

TONY

I promise you, I will not forget.

(SHE WALKS AWAY FROM HIM)

TONY

(LOOKS FOR JOE AND WALKS TOWARD HIM)

Joe, forget about BANUCHI tonight. We will take care of that later. Right now, I want to know who is handling our legal matters and if we have a couple of good doctors on our payroll.

JOE

Our lawyer is Bernstein and his son, the son is better than his father you remember him but doctors? What do you want doctors for? Are you sick or something?

TONY

Well, after tonight, after this get-together, someone out there has already called the cops. I am surprised they are not here already, but that's their problem. Regarding the lawyer and doctors, I mean psychiatry, it's very simple. As soon as I show my face, the feds and the cops are going to pick me up. The first question is, where have you been in the last 20 years? The answer, I don't remember; I had amnesia. That's where the doctors come in. So first thing tomorrow, you call Bernstein and tell him you need to see him; nothing on the phone. When you see him, then you set up a meeting at RUDY'S transportation company with us. That way, if the cops pick me up, I will have my lawyer with me, and what about my apartment? Also, you will be driving me around until I get my driver's license. I am not giving them one inch so that they can pin me with anything.

JOE

The apartment was fully furnished yesterday, so tomorrow, you and I will take all your personal stuff over there so you can get settled in. By the way, it's in the upper west side. This will do for now until we set you up in a better place.

TONY

Well, that's settled. What do you say if we enjoy ourselves and see how things are taken shape around here?

CHAPTER 10

POLICE HEADQUARTERS
MONDAY MORNING

BILL GONZALEZ......TASK FORCE NYC.

Good morning COSTELLO. How was your weekend?

COSTELLO

Nothing much, but Sgt. JACOB tells me there was a big party at Mulberry Street. All the big shots were there. One of the pigeons call him about it, and he told him to get him as many plate numbers as he could. He calls his Captain, but he told him to forget about it they were probably looking for their new Don in a whisky bottle.

GONZALEZ SHOUTS

WHAT DO YOU MEAN there was a party at Mulberry and no one looked into it?

WHATS WRONG WITH JACOB AND HIS CAPTAIN? WHAT DO THEY WANT FOR THE CRIME BOSSES?

SEND THEM A LETTER AND LET THEM KNOW WHAT THEY ARE GOING TO DO NEXT!

IS TRAVES IN THE BUILDING? FIND JACOB WHEREVER HE IS AND HAVE HIM CALL ME.

(Gonzalez receives a call on his cell phone)

Hello Gonzalez here.

NICKY SANTINI IS EXCITED

GONZALEZ, THIS IS NICKY SANTINI. I HAVE SOME INFORMATION ABOUT A BIG PARTY AT MULBERRY ST. SATURDAY NIGHT, BUT IT WILL COST YOU SEVERAL TWENTIES, I MEAN ONE HUNDRED. IT'S ABOUT THE NEW DON.

GONZALEZ

O.K. we have a deal spill it.

NICKY

There is a new DON, never heard his name until now must be out of town.

GONZALEZ

Cut the crap and tell me his name if you want the money.

NICKY

His name is Tony DEFEO. You ever hear that name, and when do I get my money?

GONZALEZ

You will get your money, but find out where he is or where I can find him.

NICKY

Hey, take it easy. What did I just do? Mention the devil or something.

GONZALEZ

Call me back when you have something.

Hangs up and calls JOE TRAVES

Hello JOE, we have a problem. I just got a call about a party at Mulberry Saturday night. Sgt. COSTELLO knew about it and he called his Captain and told him to forget it. Guess what the party was about? We have a New Mafia Boss and his name is MR. TONY DEFEO.

JOE

You get that fucking Sgt. and his Captain in my office by the time I get down there, got it?

(HANGS UP)

NANCY

JOE, what's wrong?

JOE

There is a new Don for The Mafia and guess who it is? The man the Mayor spoke to me about, the missing gangster, MR. TONY DEFEO. Mom, leave me the dinner in the oven. I will not be home early.

(JOE WALKS OUT)

NANCY

DOES NOT SAY A WORD; SHE CAN NOT BELIEVE WHAT HER SON JUST TOLD HER. AFTER SO MANY YEARS, HE HAS COME BACK INTO HER LIFE. STILL, JOE AND TONY AGAINST EACH OTHER; THIS CANNOT BE HAPPENING TO HER. SHE SITS DOWN AND GOES BACK TO HER TEEN YEARS WHEN SHE MET TONY AT CHURCH. HE WAS AN ALTAR BOY AND STARTS LOOKING IN HER ALBUM OF HER JUNIOR HIGH SCHOOL YEARS, LOOKING FOR SOMEONE SHE COULD CALL IF IT IS TRUE THAT TONY IS ALIVE, BUT WHO SHE HAS NOT HAD CONTACT WITH ANYONE FROM HER PAST SINCE SHE LEFT TONY.

CHAPTER 11

JOE TRAVES IS DRIVING TO
POLICE HEADQUARTERS MAKES A CALL

Commissioner, this is JOE Travis. I told GONZALEZ to have 2 of your men in my office. I need to speak with them. I need you to make sure that they are there. The names are SGT.JACOB and his CAPTAIN. I hope that you also be there, or by the way, the reason for the meeting is that we have a new DON for the Mafia in the USA. His name is TONY DEFEO.

COMIMISSIONER

What are you talking about? Who told you this?

JOE

You just give me 10 minutes to get to your office and you will find out. (HANGS UP)

JOE TRAVES OFFICE

JOE

Gonzalez, did you get the Captain and the sergeant?

GONZALEZ

They're waiting in your office.

JOE

Call the Commissioner's office and let him know we are waiting for him and his men are here also.

JOE

GOOD MORNING, I AM JOE TRAVES, FBI. TASK FORCE IN NEW YORK CITY.

CAPTAIN

I am Captain SANTINI and he is SGT.JACOBS, what are we doing here? We received a call from the POLICE CHIEF Office right after Gonzalez called us to come down here, so would you mind telling me what this is all about?

JOE

Calm down, Captain and hear me out. Can you tell me why you did not follow up on the tip the SGT. got at the Mulberry Street party on Saturday night?

CAPTAIN

I told the SGT. to get as many plate numbers as possible so we could know who was there.

And to forget it, they were just trying to find their new Don in a whisky bottle.

So, what did I do wrong, we have a lot in the streets and I was not going to send my men to some party of the Mafia?

JOE

Well, for starters, that party was for the celebration of the new Don for the Mafia in the USA.

In other words, you let go by your hands for us to make a raid for whatever trump-up charge, and we would have had in our hands a man that disappeared over 20 years ago, and you let him go.

Is that a good enough reason for you being here now? I want you and your Sgt. to contact all your stoolies and find out where this guy is.

COMMISSIONER

I have heard everything, so you two get the hell out of here and find out where MR. DEFEO is and Captain you will call MR. TRAVES and let him know what you find out, and I want to see you and SGT.JACOBS in my office tomorrow at 8 A.M. sharp. Now get the hell out of here.

JOE

Gonzalez, call your man and tell him he has 100 bucks plus what you owe him if he can tell you where we can pick up MR. DEFEO.

CHAPTER 12

AT THE SAME TIME IN TONY DEFEO APT. IN THE WEST SIDE

JOE

TONY, Bernstein wants to know where you want to see him so you two can talk.

TONY

You tell BERSTEIN to be at RUDY's place at 1 O'CLOCK, and I want you to pass the word that the New Don is going to be at RUDY's place today in the afternoon. That way, I will be picked up by the cops or the feds and get this thing over so we can deal with what we have to do; they will be happy and we can go along with what we have to do.

JOE SPEAKS OUT LOUD

I WILL GET THE WORD OUT, SO EVERY STOOLIE IN NEW YORK KNOWS WHERE YOU ARE GOING TO BE TODAY AT 1 O CLOCK.

(AT THE SAME TIME AT JOE TRAVES OFFICE)

JOE TRAVES

GONZALEZ, I want you to get me everything we have on this MR. DEFEO and I mean everything— friends and also pictures on this guy updated. I want to know who we are going to pick up. We don't know what this guy looks like. Get on it fast.

(ONE HOUR LATER)

NICKY SANTINI MAKES A PHONE CALL TO GONZALEZ

Hello GONZALEZ, I think I found your man. Something is happening at GRACIANO TRUCKING ON MULBERRY ST. The word is the BIG MAN IS COMING DOWN HERE TODAY, so I found your mystery man.

GONZALEZ SPEAKS LOUD

DO YOU HAVE ANY IDEA WHEN HE WILL BE THERE OR IS HE THERE ALREADY?

SANTINI

I will call you as soon as I see or hear anything happen.

GONZALEZ IS EXCITED

I WILL BE DOWN THERE IN TWENTY MINUTES. I WILL CALL YOU AS SOON AS I AM ON MOTT STREET. HANGS UP.

GONZALEZ

JOE, the big boy is going to be at GRACIANO TRUCKING AT MULBERRY. I JUST GOT A CALL FROM SANTINI.

JOE YELLS

DID YOU GET THE PICTURES OF HIM?

GONZALEZ EXCITED

THEY JUST CAME IN ON THE SCANNER. LET ME MAKE SEVERAL COPIES, AND WE WILL KNOW WHO TO LOOK FOR.

JOE YELLS

GONZALEZ, DON'T FORGET TO INTERCEPT THE PHONES AT GRACIANOS PLACE, SO WE WILL KNOW WHAT'S GOING ON. GET THE TRUCK DOWN THERE FAST AND FIRST INTERCEPT THE PHONES, THEN GET THE COURT ORDER. WE DON'T HAVE TIME TO LOSE. MOVE IT.

GONZALEZ

Will get the truck down there first and set up the stake out then, call the judge for the court order.

(MEANWHILE AT TONYS APARTMENT)

JOE starts to speak low then raises his voices

TONY, let's get moving. I want to get to RUDY'S place before BERNSTEIN. I WANT TO CHECK OUT WHO IS INTERESTED in WHATS GOING ON AT RUDY'S PLACE TODAY. I THINK I KNOW WHO IT COULD BE, BUT I WANT TO BE SURE!

TONY

Well, let's get this over with. Let's lead the cops. Have their 4 of JULY with me; let's see what they will charge me, but let's get the party rolling.

CHAPTER 13

**RUDY'S PLACE ON MULBERRY STREET
(THE FEDS HAVE COMPLETED THEIR
SURVEILLANCE ON RUDY'S PLACE)
TONY AND JOE ARRIVE AT RUDY'S PLACE THEY
ARE MET BY RUDY AND ORSINI**

NICKY SANTINI MAKES A CALL TO GONZALEZ

Hello GONZALEZ! Mr. Big just arrived at RUDY'S Place. If you want to get him, you better move fast. What about my money, all of it?

GONZALEZ

I will call you later and meet you at NINOS PLACE at 47 street and Third Avenue O.K.

GONZALEZ

JOE, MR. DEFEO arrived at RUDY'S PLACE.

JOE

Well, let's pick up MR. DEFEO and see where he has been in the last 25 years.

(INSIDE RUDY'S PLACE)

JOE

TONY, this is BERNSTEIN.

TONY

CONSULAR IS EVERYTHING SET LIKE I WANT?

BERNSTEIN SPEAKS A LITTLE LOUD, HE HAD NEVER SEEN TONY UNTIL NOW

EVERYTHING IS JUST THE WAY YOU WANT, AND I HAVE 3 DOCTORS ON STAND BY, AND I MUST TELL YOU I HAVE TO HAND IT TO YOU. IT'S A GREAT IDEA, NOW JUST SIT BACK AND LET'S SEE WHAT HAPPEN'S NEXT.

JOE TRAVES

GONZALEZ, call our surveillance team. If anyone tries to leave that place before we arrive, they are ordered to move in and detain everyone until we get there, which should be in twenty minutes.

GONZALEZ IS EXCITED

I AM ON IT, JOE. NOW, LET'S GET DOWN THERE AND GET THIS GUY.

(JOE TRAVES ARRIVES AT GRACIANOS PLACE AND ALL THE AGENTS COME OUT. JOE WALKS INTO THE OFFICE OF GRACIANO)

JOE

MR. GRACIANO, I am federal agent JOE TRAVES. I am looking for TONY DEFEO. I understand he is here.

GRACIANO

Sure, he's here, he is in his office. He works here. Is anything wrong officer?

JOE

TAKE ME TO HIM............ **THEY WALK TOWARD AN OFFICE THEY ENTER!**

JOE SHOUTS

YOU, TONY DEFEO!

TONY

Yes, I AM TONY DEFEO!

JOE SHOUTS

I AM FEDERAL AGENT, JOE TRAVES, AND YOU ARE UNDER ARREST!

TONY

What have I done?

JOE RAISES HIS VOICE

Well, to begin WITH, I WANT TO KNOW WHERE YOU HAVE BEEN FOR THE LAST TWENTY OR MORE YEARS!

TONY

Well, Agent TRAVES, I don't know where I have been. I have had some kind of amnesia. I can only tell you about the last 4 or 5 weeks. The rest is a total blank. I don't remember nothing.

BERNSTEIN

Excuse me, Agent TRAVES, but MR. DEFEO will be admitted to a hospital for medical observation due to his loss of memory and as far as I know, losing your memory is not a crime, much less a federal crime. I am an attorney at law, and I am his legal representative. If it is necessary and if that is the only charge you have against him, I am afraid it will have to wait because the Doctor is waiting for him at ST. VINCENT'S for some medical test.

TONY

I will be more than happy to help you Agent TRAVES and that way, I will find out where I have been for the last years. Who better than the federal government to help me solve this mystery?

BERNSTEIN

Agent TRAVES, the moment that MR. DEFEO is let out of the hospital, I will call you so you will tell me at what time you want him in your office, and we will be there to answer all the questions MR. DEFEO is able to.

(JOE TRAVES AND HIS MAN WALK OUT OF THE OFFICE)

TONY

Writes in a paper real fast and shows it to everyone, **THE PLACE COULD BE BUG DO NOT SAY A WORD.**

JOE TRAVES

GONZALEZ, put a tail on MR. DEFEO. Put men inside the hospital. Now get on it fast and put a wire in his room, so you make sure he gets the right room and I want to know where he is living.

TONY

Consular, let's get down to the hospital to begin the test and maybe, I can remember something of the past. Call the DOCTOR and make sure everything is ready. I don't want to be there more than I have to, one or two days at the most.

Chapter 14

ST. VICENT HOSPITAL

TONY AND MR. BERNSTEIN ARRIVED AT THE HOSPITAL THEY WERE MET BY A DOCTOR

DR. ROBERT GOBEL

Hello BERNSTEIN. I have all the paperwork ready.

BERNSTEIN

TONY, this is DR. GOBEL.

TONY

My pleasure, DOCTOR GOBEL. Will these tests take long and how long will I be here? I hope it will not take more than one or two days.

DOCTOR GOBEL

Well, let's get you to your room first and have you change your clothes, and we can start with one or two of the lab tests.

That will leave me with just three other tests, two we will do first thing in the morning and the last one we have to do Tuesday, after that you can leave the hospital the rest we can do in my office if it's all right with you.

TONY

The faster we get this over, the faster I get out of here.

(TONY IS TAKEN TO HIS ROOM AND TAKEN FOR HIS TEST LATER IN HIS ROOM)

JOE

TONY, the DOCTOR told me you should be ready by noon so I will be here by 10: A.M. so you finish here and we get the hell out of here.

TONY

You call BERNSTEIN and tell him to set up the meeting with the federal agent TRAVES for Wednesday. I want to get that over as soon as possible...HE WRITES ON A PAPER...BE CAREFUL WHAT YOU SAY.

JOE

I will take care of everything, and by the way, ORSINI is coming over to keep you company tonight.

He is afraid something will happen to you. He should be over in a little while. At least you will have someone to talk to.

ORSINI WALKS INTO THE ROOM

ORSINI

TONY, how are you? Is everything O.K.? Anything you need?

TONY

Everything is O.K. Just take a seat and enjoy yourself.

NURSE WALKS INTO THE ROOM

MR. DEFEO, will you please come with me? We have some test for you.

TONY

I am all yours, madam. ORSINI, you stay here and watch everything until I come back.

2 HOURS LATER

TONY RETURN'S TO THE ROOM

TONY

Anyone visit me while I was out ORSINI.

ORSINI

Nobody except the maintenance men who came to check something's nobody else.

TONY

ORSINI let's take a walk and see this place.

ONCE OUTSIDE

TONY

Watch out for what you say once we are in the room again.

Did you see what the guy did inside the room? He probably place a bug or two, so be careful when we are back in the room. Meanwhile, let's go to the cafeteria and eat something.

BACK AT JOE TRAVES OFFICE

JOE

GONZALES is everything set at the hospital.

GONZALES

The room is bugged, and the phone is tapped, so let's wait and see what happens next.

PHONE RING'S

GONZALES here or sure, JOE, your mother.

JOE

Hi mom, is something wrong?

NANCY

No, nothing is wrong. I just wanted to see if you are O.K. You left the house so mad. Did you arrest the man?

JOE

No, I did not, couldn't do anything. As a matter of fact, he is going to be in the hospital for a couple of days. I have to wait until he is out to see him in my office with his attorney, but I finally met the mystery man the famous MR. DEFEO.

NANCY

Hospital? What hospital? Did something happen to him? Is he sick?

JOE

No, he is not sick. He is at ST. VINCENTS Hospital for some tests. He claims he has had amnesia for the last twenty-five years. Can you believe a lie that big?

NANCY

He must be some sort of a man to come up with a story like that, I will leave your food in the oven, and I am glad you finally met your mystery man. See you later. Goodbye.

NANCY STARTS TO THINK, IS IT REALLY TONY COMING BACK FROM THE DEAD AFTER ALL THESE YEARS, AND ONLY TONY COULD COME UP WITH A STORY LIKE THAT. I HAVE TO CALL THE HOSPITAL AND SEE IF IT REALLY IS HIM, BUT LET ME THINK ABOUT IT. SHE PICKS UP THE PHONE AND CALLS INFORMATION FOR THE HOSPITAL NUMBER, WRITES IT DOWN AND STARTS TO THINK AGAIN ABOUT WHAT SHE SHOULD DO. SHE DECIDES, SHE DIALS THE NUMBER.

Hello, could you connect me with MR. TONY DEFEO room please.

ORSINI

Hello.

NANCY

Could you please put TONY ON THE PHONE?

ORSINI

He just steps out a minute. Hold the line, TONY someone on the phone for you.

TONY

I will be in a moment, whoever it is to hold for a minute.

ORSINI

He will be right in, don't hang up.

NANCY

I will wait.

CHAPTER 15

MEANWHILE AT JOE TRAVES OFFICE

GONZALES

JOE, a woman just called DEFEO. They are tracing the call. It's somewhere in the upper west side.

JOE

Don't lose it let's see who she is. Who knows that MR. DEFEO IS IN THE HOSPITAL.

MEANWHILE AT THE HOSPITAL

Hello TONY here, hello.

NANCY

Is this TONY DEFEO, JULIA DEFEO SON?

TONY RAISES HIS VOICE

YES, I AM JULIA DEFEO SON. WHO IS THIS? HELLO, SAY SOMETHING. WHAT DO YOU WANT? WHO IS THIS? HEY ORSINI, WHO WAS THIS ON THE PHONE? SHE HAS A NAME OR SOMETHING?

ORSINI

No, she just asks for you, nothing more.

TONY

Who would call me at the hospital just to ask me if I am JULIA DEFEO's son, somebody that knows me but nobody knows I am here and why the call?

JOE TRAVES OFFICE

GONZALEZ

JOE, we did not have enough time to ID the phone, but it is in the perimeter where you live. We will check and see if we have anyone in that area who is connected to these people.

AT THE HOSPITAL

TONY

ORSINI, when are you leaving or do you have time for a card game?

ORSINI

I have all the time in the world. I am not leaving here tonight just in case, so sit down and start dealing, and don't you worry, you can sleep like a baby. I will be here and no buts about it. I am not taking any chances of something happening to you after so many years without seeing you.

NEXT DAY IN TONY DEFEO ROOM

NURSE SMITH

Good morning, MR. DEFEO! They are waiting for you at the lab for your test. Would you please sit in this wheelchair so we can get started?

TONY

I am yours to command. I want to get out of here more than you could ever imagine. So, drive on and get this over as soon as possible so I can get out of this hospital faster than you can say, Jackie Robinson. So drive on, my faithful nurse.

ORSINI

I will stay here just in case someone calls you.

2 HOURS LATER, TONY IS RETURNED TO HIS ROOM

ORSINI

Is everything O.K. TONY? Can we get out of this place now?

TONY

Yes, we can get out of here. Call JOE and tell him to call BERNSTEIN to set up the meeting with the FEDERAL agent for tomorrow if it can be done so, we can get that over with and I can get on with my life if they let me.

JOE TRAVES OFFICE

GONZALEZ

TRAVES, the Don is leaving the hospital in a little while. He calls his friend to call the lawyer and for him to call you and see if DEFEO can come over tomorrow for the meeting with you. What are you going to do?

JOE

Let him call. I know what I am going to tell the counselor.

ORSINI

JOE , this is ORSINI. We are getting out of here in a little while. TONY said to call BERNSTEIN and try to set up the meeting for this afternoon.

JOE

All right tell, TONY I will take care of it.

MAKES THE CALL

Hello BERNSTEIN, JOE PAGANO here. TONY is leaving the hospital soon and said for you to try and set the meeting for tomorrow. Call me back and let me know what they say.

BERNSTEIN

I will try, but I don't think that the federal agent is going for a meeting when TONY decides. I will call you back and let you know.

MAKES THE CALL

JOE TRAVES OFFICE

GONZALEZ

JOE ON LINE 2, MR. BERNSTEIN.

TRAVES here. What can I do for you, counselor? Is anything wrong with MR. DEFEO at the hospital?

BERNSTEIN

No, everything is fine. It is that MR. DEFEO is leaving the hospital tomorrow, and I was wondering if we could have that meeting tomorrow afternoon.

JOE

No counselor, not tomorrow. I want you and MR. DEFEO in my office Thursday at 1:P.M. and bring with you all the medical test results and the DOCTORS' medical opinion on MR. DEFEO case. Make sure you have copies of what you bring because what you bring stays here, understood?

BERNSTEIN

Understood very well, MR. TRAVES. Tell you what, I know I will not have those medical records by Thursday. Let's say we get together Friday at 1:P. M. if it's all right with you.

JOE

No problem with me. You call me early and let me know. If I am not here you speak with my partner GONZALEZ and leave the message, and don't forget what you bring stays with me, counselor.

BERNSTEIN CALLS JOE

JOE, this is BERNSTEIN. The meeting is for Friday at 1 P.M. I need time to get the medical records. This guy wants; he is no pushover. I will talk to you later. Right now, I have to talk to the DOCTORS IN PERSON and will contact you later.

JOE

Hello ORSINI, it's JOE. I will be there in 30 minutes in front of the hospital. I will be in a different car. Keep an eye out for me. I will explain everything to TONY when I see him.

CHAPTER 16

IN FRONT OF HOSPITAL

ORSINI

TONY, the car is here let's get out of here fast.

(They come out of hospital and get into the car)

TONY

JOE, what did BERNSTEIN tell you?

JOE

The meeting is on Friday. This guy wants your medical records and the DOCTORS' opinion on your case. He is after you. BERNSTEIN is getting set for Friday.

Tony

Why the car changes?

JOE

Just in case my car has been bugged, I decided to make a switch just to play it safe where we are going.

TONY

I am sure we are being tailed by one of TRAVES men, so call MR.BANUCHI and tell him to be at GINOS place. I want to see him after that. I want to see BIG SAM up in Harlem and also SPANISH REY, both at the same time. What I have to say it's for both of them, but first we have to convince MR. TRAVES men that I am at GINOS place, so as soon as we arrive, you will slip out thru the tunnel, go to RUDY place and get another car for us.

Contact BIG SAM AND SPANISH REY that I am going uptown to see them tonight. After your set, come back the same way. And after I finish with MR. BANUCHI, we slip out and go uptown and see BIG SAM AND SPANISH REY and get that out of the way, and tomorrow we start organizing. First thing, the old man casinos, we need money fast. Park the car in front of Ginos place, so Traves men will think we are inside as long as they see the car there.

INSIDE GINOS PLACE, YOUNG BANUCHI IS WAITING AT THE BAR

TONY

Good afternoon, MR. BANUCHI. Wait until JOE lets you know to slip into the back room, understood?

BANUCHI

Yes, DON DEFEO.

JOE waits 15 minutes and sends BANUCHI.

BANUCHI GOES THROUGH THE TUNNEL AND FINDS TONY DEFEO WAITING FOR HIM

TONY

Take a seat MR. BANUCHI. I hear that the young Turks look at you as their leader and that you're very ambitious. There is nothing wrong with that except if you are very young and very ambitious and you think you know everything it takes to run an organization of this magnitude.

It can earn you an early GRAVE. Get the picture BANUCHI. I promise your mother that I will have a talk with you and that everything will be O.K. So, you behave yourself and don't be stupid and learn and I will find out why the old man like you so much and that way I will not have to break my promise to your mother about anything happening to you. Give me a chance to see what you have and how you can fit in with what I have in mine. So, it's up to you to go up in the ranks just like I did or you dig yourself an early grave. Do we understand each other?

BANUCHI

You will have no problems with me, DON DEFEO. Anything else I need to know?

TONY

No, nothing for the moment except keep your boys in line. I DON'T want any problems with the cops or anyone else, understood?

BANUCHI

Understood perfectly, DON DEFEO.

TONY

Go back to the club and tell JOE and ORSINI to come down and don't forget to give my regards to your mother.

BANUCHI GETS UP AND RETURNS TO GINOS PLACE.

JOE, the DON said for you and ORSINI to slip out and go to him he is waiting for you.

JOE

Everything square away with the Young Turk BANUCHI.

TONY

I hope so. I would hate to break my promise to NANIA, but you know something, JOE. Something about that kid makes me like him, and I only have seen him 3 times. With tonight, well, let's get to work, JOE. Go back to the club, give your car keys to RUDY and tell him that in about 30 minutes, have 5 or 6 of the guys go out; 3 of them to get in the car. Make sure that fed, who is on our tail, does not see who gets in the car and for them to take a ride to Brooklyn or queens, and that way, the guy will think he is following us. We get free of that agent. I don't want them to know where I have been tonight; it might wake up agent TRAVES curiosity. I don't think he needs much for that to happen, so go to RUDY so we can get out of here fast.

JOE GOES BACK TO THE CLUB, TALKS TO RUDY AND COMES BACK AND HEADS FOR HARLEM

TONY

JOE, where is the meeting going to take place?

JOE

I set it up at FRANK MARTINO restaurant, it's a safe place; if something were to happen, we can get out fast and safe, something like back in the neighborhood. BIG SAM and SPANISH REY should be there by now. Let me call FRANK. Hello FRANK, this is JOE. Is BIG SAM and SPANISH REY there already?

FRANK

Yes, they're here, arrived a couple of minutes ago.

JOE

Send them to the back room we are almost in front of your place. See you soon.

FRANK TALKS TO THEM AND THEY BOTH GO TO THE BACK ROOM THAT IS SAFE

CHAPTER 17

FRANK MARTINO PLACE

TONY, JOE, AND ORSINI PULL UP IN FRONT OF THE PLACE, GET OUT OF THE CAR, AND WALK IN

JOE

Hello FRANK, long time don't see each other. How is the family? This is TONY DEFEO. I think you hear about him by now.

FRANK

My pleasure MR. DEFEO, please follow me. ORSINI, where have you been? Don't you like my cooking anymore?

ORSINI

I love your cooking, but I have been very busy since TONY got back, but I'll tell you what, let's see if we can come back, the 3 of us, and you prepare something special for TONY, so he will know why this place is so good.

THEY WALK INTO THE BACK ROOM

JOE

BIG SAM AND SPANISH REY, this is TONY DEFEO, you know him by reference already, but here he is.

TONY

My pleasure, BIG SAM. JOE has spoken very well of you. I hope we can become good friends like you and JOE and everything will be just like when the old man was here. If everything works out, it will be much better for everyone, but I will explain later on.

SPANISH REY I used to know your father very well. We had good times. Him and me, we had a very good and sincere friendship, and if you are half the man your father was, we will get along just fine.

Now let's get down to our business. As you both know, since the old man was sent away, everything has crumbled, and I was asked to come back by the commission, not to replace the old man because nobody replaces him. But the company has to be put in order so that we all benefit from this business that we are in. The first thing I want from both of you is a list of all the cops, politicians, and other people who have taken bribes from you in this part of the city. Since the old man is not here to tell me who they are, I need the information from you two. The reason for this is we are going to take the heat away from us, but first, we are going to put some heat on some of these respectable people. The second reason I am here is that I need both of you to start paying your 20 percent just like it has always been. You two were the last people that I had to speak with so everything would be crystal clear and to get things straight. Are there any questions any doubts? Well, your silence means that ORSINI can call FRANK to bring us a couple of bottles of wine to celebrate and anything else you desire to drink. I don't normally do this, but the occasion is worth it.

SPANISH REY

TONY, we are having a lot of problems not just from the cops on our gambling, but the Columbians and the Jamaicans are also trying to move in since the DON was sent away, what should we do now fight back or wait for you.

TONY

You are truly your father's son. Spoken just like he would have if he were here. Hold back both of you, give me some time to try to get some cops on my payroll and let them do the work for us. Also, I have to try and talk to these people. If words don't work with them, I will set an example but call JOE if it gets too rough but today is TUESDAY. I will have JOE contact whoever it is and set up a meeting no later than THURSDAY because tomorrow and Friday I will be busy and it cannot be put off. So, if BIG SAM does not have anything to say I will have one more glass of wine and leave you people to enjoy the rest, I have other pending matters to care off.

CHAPTER 18

TRAVES AGENT CALLS TRAVES AT HOME

Hello TRAVES! This is agent Carson. I am tailing DEFEO to Queens, he stops at MULBERRY ST. at GINOS place for a while and I am following him. Let's see where they take me. I will call if anything happens.

TRAVES

You call me if the slightest thing happens. Take care of yourself.

NANCY

Who was that on the phone, JOE? One of your men?

TRAVES

Yeah, mom, he's tailing MR. DEFEO and by the way, I did not tell you that on Friday, I will have MR. DEFEO in my office with his lawyer. He has to bring me all his test results along with his DOCTOR'S report on his supposed loss of memory, so I will have MR.BIG face-to-face. I am really looking forward to that meeting and maybe I will get an idea why the Mayor.

Thinks so highly of this man who is nothing more than a criminal who should be in jail with the Don, but he better watches his step because I am out to put him behind bars.

NANCY

JOE, why do you hate this man so much? You don't know anything about him, yet you want to send him to prison.

JOE LIFTS HIS VOICE

MOM, THIS MAN IS THE BOSS OF THE MAFIA IN THE USA. He is no little two-bit gangster. He is the boss. If I did not know you better, I would think you are in his favor against me.

NANCY

JOE, for GODS sake, how could you say something like that? Let's change this conversation; we are getting nowhere with this. I am going to bed, goodnight, JOE. I love you very much.

JOE

I love you very much also, sweetheart and don't you worry about a man that you don't even know. Goodnight, mother. Sleep well.

NANCY starts thinking

This cannot be happening, JOE is after TONY. This cannot happen. What can I do to stop this? Who can I go to? She goes to bed hoping that tomorrow she will have a solution.

CHAPTER 19

MEANWHILE, IN JOE PAGANO CAR

TONY

JOE, let's call it a night as far as business is concerned. Take me someplace where we can have a couple of drinks and you and ORSINI can fill me in on these Columbians and Jamaican gangs. I have a feeling they are going to be a pain and I don't want no violence until we are set but let's have that drink. By the way, JOE did you find the person I want for the electronic service? I want to meet him. I want him to understand he will only take orders from you ORSINI or me nobody else.

JOE

I will call him right now and set up the meeting for tomorrow and let me call JUAN PEREZ. He is the Columbian with the biggest gang and the rest will follow him, so I will set it up for Thursday and the Jamaicans, we can handle them if they get out of hand. So, TONY, we are almost set.

TONY

By the way, call some place where we can stay tonight. I am sure that TRAVES is finding out where I am staying and if he has already found out, they are waiting for me. So, call some place a hotel where we are going to stay tonight. I have three things pending, and I don't want the feds to know about it so make the call and call your wife that you're not coming home tonight. If she does not believe you, put me on the phone. Make sure you use the right cell phone. After that, call your friend in the electronics field and don't forget the reservations. Start with a call to your wife. Also, do you have the list on all the people I ask you for, especially the cops because I want to put some heat on the Columbians but I want the cops to do it for us. That way, nobody can point the finger at us for the time being. After we are set, I will take care of them in my own special way and put them in their place once and for all. As a matter of fact, the cops are going to put them out of circulation for us, so get me the list and also call BIG SAM and SPANISH REY. I need their list for tomorrow so I can put the electronics man to work fast. I do not want anything pending when I see this agent TRAVES on Friday afternoon because we start rolling the moment I step out of his office. So, start making your calls and then we relax for a while I hope.

JOE

I will get on it as soon as we arrive at SAMMY's place on 5 AVE. You will like him. He runs a tight ship; you relax with ORSINI and, I will take care of my part and get back to you fast.

CHAPTER 20

THEY ARRIVE AT SAMMY PLACE

JOE

SAMMY, I have to make several phone calls that are private. By the way, this is TONY DEFEO.

SAMMY

You go to NELSON and tell him I said to give you all you need, DON DEFEO. It is an HONOR to have you here. I imagine you will like a private boot for you and your friends, soundproof if possible.

TONY

SAMMY, I am beginning to think this could be the start of a good and long friendship.

SAMMY

Come this way, nobody will bother you, I assure you of that. I run this place like a captain runs his ship tight, so no nuts come loose what do you wish to drink?

TONY

I will have rum with coke and lemon and for ORSINI whatever he wants. ORSINI, we three have not been together like today for more than 25 years. So, let's celebrate for the good old times and for the good future years ahead of us after Friday. Let's wait for JOE, so we can make that old toast we used to make all for three until death separates us. Those were good old days but let's live the present and try to forget the past.

JOE

TONY, first my wife sends her best, she wants you over, so you can meet your GOD child and she is dying to see you. You are also invited ORSINI. In regard to the rest, the electronic expert will be here tomorrow. I think it is safer here than any other place for the moment at 10: A.M., I also made some calls and the list that is pending will be in my hands by tomorrow here also by 10: A.M.

I will speak with SAMMY.

So the place is open and only him here and in regard to the COLUMBIANS their boss wants to meet you and I think more than you want to meet him. Let's see what he has in his mind. What we do not know never hurts to learn what bothers your enemy, and in regard to Harlem both BIG SAM and SPANISH REY are sending their list by runner, but not here. I am going to ask SAMMY for his help, SAMMY come over here. I need you to send one or two of your men to pick up something for me, they have to be careful not to be followed back here, it could be the cops or the feds, understand?

SAMMY

You can rest assured they will not be followed back here by anyone. Now come with me, so you will give them the details.

Where will they pick up your package? I will give them my instructions on what they will do so they will not be tailed.

JOE SPEAKS TO SAMMY MEN AND THEY LEAVE

JOE

SAMMY, I need you to make reservations for 3 at one of the hotels near here, but not put it under our names. Make it until Friday and we will be meeting a person here tomorrow at 10: A.M., I need you to be here but nobody else and Thursday, we will be meeting some people and I need a private and safe place for that meeting. I can tell you TONY does not forget loyalty.

SAMMY

JOE, you know me for many years and you know you can trust me just like the old DON used too. I miss the old man. I hope everything works out for the new DON. I will call my cousin at the hotel and make the reservation for 3. Anything else I can do for you?

JOE

Yeah, don't change and I will be with TONY AND ORSINI waiting for your men to come back. When they return take them to the back and call me.

JOE RETURNS TO THE TABLE

JOE

Well, TONY, everything is falling into place. Once we get the list, we can put the electronics expert to work, so let's sit back and wait for SAMMY's men to get back.

TONY

Speaking of SAMMY, who is he?

JOE

He has a lot of connections. The old man liked him a lot and he was very loyal to the old man. He can be trusted. Time will tell you I am right, but the old man trusted him, and you of all people, know that getting the old man to trust was not easy just like it is with you.

SAMMY

JOE, my men are back. Come with me.

JOE GOES WITH SAMMY TO A BACK ROOM AND GIVES THE PACKAGE

JOE

Are you sure you were not followed?

THE MAN

No, because I was not the one that picked up the package, we made a switch following SAMMY's instructions.

JOE

Well, take this and split it evenly between the three, and I will not forget what you did. Some things do not just get paid off with money, I'll be seeing you take care.

JOE WALKS TOWARDS THE TABLE WHERE TONY IS

JOE

TONY, here is our package. I think we should check this when we are at the hotel.

TONY

Definitely, I never mix business with liquor and this requires all of my attention and yours and ORSINI too.

SAMMY

JOE, everything at the hotel is set when you and your party are ready. Two of my men will take you out the back way and drive you there. That way, nobody but me knows where you are. Say anything you need at the hotel, call my cousin. He is the manager.

TONY

No, SAMMY, nothing more. I think you have covered all the bases. Now I know why the old man trusted you, and you remind me of someone ME. I will not forget this; let's get out of here. Call your men, SAMMY. We are leaving, we have work to do. See you tomorrow.

CHAPTER 21

TONY, JOE AND ORSINI ARRIVE AT THE HOTEL

ONCE IN THE ROOM

TONY

JOE, I want the electronics man to place bugs and I want him to intercept the phones of the cops and politician's in the BRONX to begin because, like I said before, I want the cops to go after the COLUMBIANS AND JAMAICANS. I do not have time for that shit; we have bigger stakes to worry about, so let's see what we have here and since you and ORSINI know who they are, you tell me who should be first. I want to see what our electronic man can do, so start reading, my friend. It's going to be a long night, but it has to be done perfectly, so let's get to work.

CHAPTER 22

NEXT MORNING, THEY ARE PICK UP AT THE HOTEL BY SAMMY MEN

SAMMY

Good morning, Mr. DEFEO. Did you all have breakfast already? If not, I will prepare something.

TONY

Good morning, SAMMY. Yes, we already had something, thank you.

SAMMY

JOE, there is a man standing outside. Is that your man.

JOE

Yes, that's him. Let him in.

JOE

Mike, how are you long time no see. I want you to meet TONY.

MIKE

My pleasure TONY.

TONY

JOE has spoken very well of you. I hope he has not exaggerated your abilities in electronics because I have a list of people that I want you to start your surveillance on them right now. In the future, you will only take orders from me, ORSINI or JOE, nobody else that is if you take the job.

MIKE

JOE was very clear of the nature of the job. I will keep my part of the deal, and we can start with the first list of people you need to have some type of surveillance and how soon you need to have some information.

TONY

I needed the information since yesterday. That's how fast I need the information on these people.

Do we understand each other? I wanted to meet you so we understood each other. I do not believe we will see each other again, but I wanted everything crystal clear between us.

MIKE

Everything is O.K. with me. I know how to do my job; I have done jobs for corporations for the secrets of their competitors.

My people are professionals in their jobs, and they keep a tight lid on what they do.

TONY

JOE, give him the list of the people we selected and that takes care of our meeting. It has been a pleasure MIKE. Have a good day.

JOE ACCOMPANIES MIKE TO THE DOOR AND SAYS GOODBYE

TONY

ORSINI, get to the nearest store and buy us some clothes. We are going to be around here until Friday, so we all need something new to wear. For me, buy me one black sports jacket, two pairs of slacks, one dark blue and the other grey and two shirts, one light blue, and the other grey. It's all on me. I hope SAMMY has a shower here because I want to shower again when you come back with the clothes.

Now for the rest of the day, we will try and see how we are financially set. I figure I would leave that for last since there is nothing we can do except use as less money as we can until we start receiving money from our different sources. That will take at least a month because that surveillance job is going to pay off, but it is also expensive. So, we have to be selective on whom we are going to be east dropping and make sure it pays off. Now I have left this for last I need you to get in touch with our accountant. Have 2 of SAMMY's men pick him up and blindfold him. Put him in the back room, and he goes out the same way, but I need to know how we are. So, get started on it; call him on a safe phone and fill SAMMY in on the importance of not being tailed. Fill me in who this guy is. If he worked for the old man, he must be good. Start talking so I have an idea with whom I will be speaking; you have the stage.

JOE

His name is ROBERT GOLDBERG. He is good and his son BOBBY is as good or better. The old man trusted them, but the old man ordered them to turn in the income report on a daily bases. In other words, the old man did not trust anyone in regard to money, except you.

TONY

Call your man and tell him I want his son also with him, I do not want any misunderstanding by father and son as to who they are dealing with. So, get on the phone don't forget a safe one.

JOE

I will take care of it now.

CHAPTER 23

MEETING WITH THE ACCOUNTANT

TWO HOURS LATER, SAMMY MEN RETURN

SAMMY

JOE, my men are back with your people there in the back. They are still blindfolded.

JOE

Keep them that way. I will be right there. Let me get TONY, he is changing his clothes. Take them to the back boot and keep them blindfolded until we get there.

JOE GETS TONY, THEY GO TO THE BOOT AND SIT DOWN

TONY

Gentlemen, you can take your blindfold off and take a seat.

JOE

Goldberg and BOBBY, sorry for the blindfold, but there are good reasons. This is TONY DEFEO, the new DON and he wanted to meet you both.

TONY

Mr. GOLDBERG, I have heard many good things about you and your son and I wanted for us to understand each other. Many things have happened since the old man was sent away. I am putting the house in order and left you for last not because you are the lease important all the contraire I want to know how we are set financially. I know the money has stopped coming in from several of our sources. Maybe some of the money that did come in is not accounted for. So bottom line is, we three start fresh from today. I am a man of few words. I like things to be crystal clear. The first mistake I forgive. If it happens again, I do not. Now that's clear, I need to know how much money I can count with. If you cannot answer me, fine. You will go back to your place and have the information for me, no later than tomorrow with a breakdown on who fell behind. That's just for my personal information. Like I said, we start a new beginning today. Any questions?

GOLDBERG

I can assure you every penny is accounted for, but I will have a full breakdown on everything for you tomorrow rest assured.

TONY

Everything will continue just the way the old man had it. JOE will fill me in on some details, but you will fill in the missing pieces tomorrow. What time do you think you will be ready? I do not want to rush you, so you tell me.

GOLDBERG

I should be finished no later than noon.

TONY

You will be picked up at 1: P.M. understood.

GOLDBERG

I will be ready.

TONY

Have the gentlemen returned to their office?

**THE MEN ARE RETURNED BY SAMMY's MEN-JOE
RETURNS TO THE TABLE**

TONY

Get in touch with MIKE and tell him I need that GOLDBERG office be wired while he is here tomorrow.

JOE

Will do it right now. That is a very good idea, TONY.

TONY

When you are finished, let's see the names on the list they sent you. I imagine there are many old names I have not heard in many years, so let's begin as soon as possible. There is a lot of work ahead for us. Wait a minute, forget about the list. For now, ask SAMMY to lend us a car.

JOE

TONY, is something wrong you feel sick or something?

TONY

No, I am not sick, it's just that a thought came to my mind. it had not crossed my mind for more than twenty years. We three are going for a drive to Staten Island, get the car and I will explain in the way. Let's get out of here.

CHAPTER 24

STATEN ISLAND

IN THE CAR, TONY EXPLAINS TO JOE AND ORSINI

TONY

JOE, you remember years ago when I would disappear with the old man for a whole day and you would ask me where was I with the old man and I always told I could not tell you? Well, the big secret was that the DON had this house in Staten Island and he would go out there and forget about everything about the business. He would try to do that at least once a month.

I guess after I left, he did not go anymore, not even once a month.

JOE

That's right, because after you left and with his son also gone, he kept to himself. He asked me to eat with him and he would start talking about you since he knew how close we three were. Come to think about it, about 4 years ago he disappeared for a day TONY, I remember because I tried to reach him and he told me he was busy and that we would meet at GINOS place at 5:P.M. and when he arrived, young BANUCHI was driving. That was the last time that I know of that he had disappeared like he used to do with you.

TONY

This BANUCHI keeps turning up on too many personal things related to the DON. What is the connection between them? What is it with this kid that the DON care for him? Turn left on exit 179 and continue until you hit the beach. There, the first house on the beach. That house belonged to his grandparents on his mother's side and it is registered under his mother maiden name. That's why the cops nor the feds know about it. I was the only one who knew about it, not even his son knew about the house. This was a special and sacred place to him. There's the house, pull over and let me go in along. I will call you it's just that I want to be along for a moment, you understand?

JOE

We understand you take your time and then call us. We will wait here; take it easy.

TONY IS IN THE HOUSE FOR ABOUT 15 MINUTES

TONY

JOE ORSINI enters into the house.

JOE

How do you feel about everything, O.K. TONY?

TONY

Just a lot of old memories, happy ones. Look what I found a lot of pictures of the old man and me. I had no idea he had these pictures. I remember he always had a man who used to take care of the place and take pictures but look, he kept them all.

JOE

TONY, the old man really loves you. All of these pictures speak for themselves.

TONY

JOE, when we get back, I want you to call BERNSTEIN to get in touch with a local lawyer from Staten Island to find out if this place owes any money on taxes or whatsoever and to pay it off. The local lawyer not BERNSTEIN and to contact a man to keep this place clean just like the old man always kept it. Come on, let's get out of here. I guess I am just like the old man for something's I am as hard as steel and things like this; I am as gentle as a kitten. Lets go there is a café up the road, we used to stop there and chew the fat.

JOE

Alright, TONY, let's go to the café, then get back to the city; we have work to do.

TONY

Forget the café and let's get back to SAMMY place and from there to the hotel, we have to work on that list tonight, so I will only have pending the COLUMBIANS before my meeting with my G-MAN friend MR. TRAVES.

THEY GET IN THE CAR AND HEAD BACK TO NEW YORK CITY, THEY ARRIVED AT SAMMY PLACE

Chapter 25

THEY ARRIVE AT THE HOTEL

JOE

SAMMY, could you have one of your men takes us to the hotel? We have a lot of work ahead of us.

SAMMY

Sure, JOE. Do you want something to eat before you go back to the hotel?

JOE

No SAMMY, we will order something at the hotel and have it brought up to our room. You can call your cousin and tell him to call me so that way we deal with him directly about anything we need and tell him. I will not forget what he has done. Anything he needs that is that you cannot handle, you let me know.

SAMMY

I will call my cousin about the food and also tell him what you just said about him. Anything else?

JOE

No, except we will see you tomorrow. Do not forget the meeting that TONY is having with the COLUMBIANS and I want you to take all of the precautions you feel necessary. I do not want surprises. Only The COLUMBIAN Boss goes to the back. I will frisk him, so you set your men up as you see fit. We will discuss that later before they arrive.

TONY ORSINI AND JOE ARE TAKEN TO THE HOTEL AND THEY START TO WORK ON THE LIST UNTIL LATE AT NIGHT.

THURSDAY MORNING, THEY STAY IN THE HOTEL UNTIL NOON THEN THEY ARE PICKED UP BY SAMMY's MEN AND TAKEN TO SAMMY's PLACE.

CHAPTER 26

SAMMY's PLACE

Sammy

Good afternoon, DON DEFEO. How do you feel JOE and ORSINI? Do you people want something to eat or drink?

TONY

No, thank you, SAMMY, but you can bring me a pot of black coffee. We have several things we have to take care before our friends arrive.

SAMMY

JOE, what time is the meeting going to take place? I have to know so, I can get set inside and outside.

JOE

I had it set up for three this afternoon so, set everything up based on that. Is the back room ready?

SAMMY

The back room is set and so will I only two men will be allowed inside with the guy, anybody else stay outside that way. I have everything covered inside and outside. Anything else I should know, Joe?

JOE

No, that covers everything, SAMMY. We are going to the back room and finish some work we have pending send us the coffee.

TONY

SAMMY, I like the way you do things. You do not like mistakes and you are a very cautious man. We have to get together after all of this is over. JOE will call you because I want to discuss with you a proposition, but that's for later let's get the COLUMBIANS out of the way first.

TONY JOE AND ORSINI GO TO THE BACK ROOM AND START TO FINISH WHAT THEY BEGAN THE NIGHT BEFORD AT THE HOTEL

TONY

JOE call BERNSTEIN and find out how we are set for tomorrow and also give him the details on the house in Staten Island No slip ups on the house. I do not want the cops nosing around that house for no reason at all and after that, call our friend and make sure he is coming.

JOE

I will take care of it. I also want to know where our COLUMBIAN friend is, I do not like to be surprised.

ORSINI

TONY, how do you feel being back in action like the old days because I am happy as hell having you back, the three of us together again.

TONY

Well, if I tell you I am not glad to be back in New York, I would be lying, but what makes it tough for me is that the old man is not here. I really miss that man. By the way, do you know if he has been told that I am back in the city and running things?

ORSINI

You will have to ask JOE on that one.

Tony

I was just thinking he would be happy but at the same time he will be asking where the hell he has been all these years.

JOE

TONY, our friend should be here any minute. SAMMY, our guest should be arriving soon.

SAMMY

No problem, JOE. We have been set for the last two hours for your information.

JOE

SAMMY, you are always one step ahead. I have to hand it to you, SAMMY. JUAN PEREZ just walks in. Go greet him and bring him back. I will take it from there. You keep your eye open for some other guest that might follow him.

CHAPTER 27

MEETING WITH COLUMBIAN BOSS

SAMMY

The doors close automatically once those three walks in; you take from here JOE, it's your party. I will make sure there are no interruptions.

JOE

Good afternoon, JUAN. Sorry for the precautions, but you can never be too careful. Come this way, TONY is waiting for you but first, let me frisk you no guns pass that door.

THEY WALK TOWARDS THE BACK ROOM TWO OF SAMMY MEN ARE STANDING IN FRONT OF THE DOOR. THEY WALK IN

JOE

JUAN, this is the new DON, TONY DEFEO.

JUAN

It is an honor to meet you, DON DEFEO. I hope after today, we will become good friends.

TONY

It is my pleasure, JUAN. I also hope that everything will be crystal clear between you and me when you leave here. I am a person of few words. As you already know, I am running things now and I am putting things together. Since the old DON went to prison, many people have done many things they should not have done. I do not want any problems with the cops or the feds for the moment until I have set everything up the way I want things to be. One of the things that I want to stop is you and your people, to stop moving in on the operations of SPANISH REY. It's not that him and BIG SAM cannot take care of themselves, it is that they are part of my organization. They follow my orders, I told them to hold back from doing anything until I spoke with you; either you are part of the organization or your against me. I don't know what your arrangement with the old DON was. I myself do not like drugs especially where kids are involved. Still, the arrangement you will explain to JOE at another time. Right know, I want to know what is your answer to what I just told you and if you understood me clearly.

JUAN

DON DEFEO, I understand you very well. You will have no problems with me or any other of the people that I am speaking for and no more problems with SPANISH REY. I give you my word.

TONY

I hope you keep your word and are responsible for any of your people getting out of hand.

We will be in touch with you to set up another meeting and discuss things in a more detailed manner. For the moment, the important situation has been resolved. Is there anything you want to ask me? If not, let's have a drink and talk about other things.

JUAN

I will have one drink and leave. I have other things to take care of.

TONY

Fine. Since everything is settled, let's have one drink and you leave.

THE DRINKS ARE BROUGHT IN, THEY DRINK AND JUAN LEAVES, AFTER HE LEAVES

TONY

JOE, I think MR.JUAN has other plans. It's not what he just said, it's what he did not say. Something is happening and he is part of it. Call SPANISH REY and tell him JUAN agreed to stop harassing, but for him to be careful the same for BIG SAM. JUAN just tipped me off because he did not ask anything about the arrangement he had; there was no interest on his part in getting to know me and what my future plans are. So, we have to find a way to get Mike to bug his phone and his office. That has to be arranged. See to it.

But first, my friend TRAVES tomorrow. Now let's have something to eat and go over that list again. I know we are missing something with those names, but we will check that out tonight. I want to be well rested for MR. TRAVES he is going to raise hell with the medical report, after tomorrow we have to be very careful, he is going after me with everything you can tell BERNSTEIN that we will pick him up, so we all arrived together.

TONY, ORSINI, AND JOE, EAT AND RETURN TO THE HOTEL, AND THEY REVIEW THE LIST UNTIL LATE THURSDAY NIGHT.

CHAPTER 28

MEANWHILE AT GINOS PLACE THURSDAY NIGHT

BANUCHI MAKES A CALL TO ONE OF HIS YOUNG TURK GANG MEMBERS

BANUCHI

SANTINI, this is BANUCHI. I want you to contact the boys. We are going to have a meeting tonight. Matter a fact, it's going to be the most important meeting of our life so, you tell everyone to get their ass down to JOE FONFRIAS place and wait for me in the back room, no liquor. I will be there in thirty minutes.

ALL OF THE YOUNG TURKS START TO ARRIVE AT JOE FONFRIAS PLACE

SANTINI

Alright you guys remember no booze and let's go to the back, BANUCHI wants us to stay there until he gets here. Don't ask me what's going on, but from the tone of his voice its big and important for us whatever it is. Wait a minute, there he is. Let's see what he has to say.

BANUCHI

Alright, boys, I had a meeting with the new DON. He wants me to keep you guys in line. He said he does not want any problems with the cops or us or anyone. He wants me to be part of his organization, whatever it is, so all of you listen, I am going to be a good boy until I have his confidence and find out what his plans are. Then we move in, so all of you be good. I have to make contact with our young friends up in Harlem, so when I make my move, they do the same uptown, so we all follow the orders that the DON gives, whether you like it or not for the time being, understand? Your silence means you understood. Now, let's have a drink to celebrate.

SANTINI

Let's drink to the future DON.

THEY ALL START TO CELEBRATE

CHAPTER 29

MEETING AT POLICE HEADQUARTERS

FRIDAY MORNING AT THE HOTEL

TONY

Joe Call BERNSTEIN and tell him we will pick him up at his office and for him to confirm the time of the meeting, so I will know when we will pick him up.

JOE

Will take care of it now. Hello Bernstein, JOE PAGANO here. We will pick you up at your office for the meeting and TONY wants you to confirm the time so we get there at the right time and not before.

BERNSTEIN

I will call and confirm that's it going to be at 1: P.M. and get back to you on it.

MAKES CALL TO TRAVES OFFICE

Hello with agent TRAVES or Gonzalez.

GONZALEZ

This is Gonzalez speaking.

BERENSTEIN

This is BERNSTEIN. I am confirming today's meeting at 1: P.M.

GONZALEZ

The meeting is on schedule. Make sure you have DEFEO medical records and do not forget, we keep them.

BERNSTEIN

I will have a copy of everything I have been given by the DOCTOR'S with their diagnosis of what happened to MR. DEFEO will see you at 1: P.M.

CALL'S JOE

JOE meeting continues at 1: P.M. call me when you are close to my office so I will be outside and we can get this over as soon as possible.

JOE

TONY, everything is set. We pick up BERNSTEIN and drive downtown to Police Headquarters to TRAVES office.

TONY

Alright let us pick up your car and pick up BERNSTEIN so I can get this meeting out of the way and we can get our business running again and making money for us.

THEY PICK UP BERNSTEIN AND DRIVE TO POLICE HEADQUARTERS

TONY

BERNSTEIN, are we ready for anything, MR. TRAVES will throw at us at this meeting?

BERNSTEIN

Tony, there is no way TRAVES nor any DOCTOR accept that what you claim is not true or possible that it happens to you. I have all the medical records to prove that it is possible and impossible to prove otherwise, so you keep quiet and let me do the talking.

TONY

Alright BERNSTEIN, you're the Ringmaster of this Circus. I will be a simple Spectator at this Circus.

CHAPTER 30

MEETING AT JOE TRAVES OFFICE

THEY ARRIVE AT POLICE HEADQUARTERS

BERSTEIN

Excuse me, where can we find agent JOE TRAVES? We have an appointment with him.

POLICEMAN

He is in office 108 on your left at the end of the hall sign here and pass through the metal detector.

BERNSTEIN

Good morning, Miss. We have an appointment with agent TRAVES. Will you please let him know that MR. BERNSTEIN and MR. DEFEO are here.

SECRETARY

MR. TRAVES, there are two gentlemen here looking for you. They say they have an appointment with you for today.

TRAVES

Show them in and take them to room 201. I will be with them shortly.

GONZALEZ

JOE, what are you going to do with the new DON?

JOE

I will let him sweat for a while I don't have nothing on him, he just disappears he does not show up no place in the USA. For the past twenty or more years, I will take his phony medical records and see if I can find something other than that, I am at a dead end for the time being, but starting now, I want a daily report on what he does every day on my desk.

I assure you as I am the son of JOE TRAVES, I am going to put MR. DEFEO in jail. Now bring them in and let us see what bull shit they have for us.

Good afternoon MR. DEFEO, how are you MR. BERNSTEIN? Are you ready to explain to me where MR. DEFEO has been for the last twenty-five years, with a convincing argument that I will certainly not believe.

MR. DEFEO I will check every corner of the USA where you could have been for the past twenty-five years and, when I do, I will know the reason of your disappearance and if there is any way, I can charge you with anything.

The old Don will have a company with the new Don, and you can rest assure that I will know what you do every minute of the day starting now, so get the hell out of my office and remember I will not rest until I put you behind bars, and leave those phony medical records, maybe they can help me put you away some day.

TONY AND BERNSTEIN GET UP AND WALK OUT WITHOUT SAYING A WORD. OUTSIDE THE BUILDING THEY ARE GREETED BY JOE AND ORSINI

Tony how did it go inside there?

TONY

MR. TRAVES, kick us out of his office and let me know, he does not believe me about my loss of memory and that he is out to put me in jail, so with that left behind, let us rebuild our organization again from coast to coast, starting with New York City. Let's start to work starting with the politicians and the police then we put our house in order.

ABOUT THE AUTHOR

He was born in Rio Piedras, Puerto Rico. He arrived at New York City at the age of 3. He grew up in the lower west side at 310 west 26 St. There he was raised by a very hard working and Strict mother. This lady raised 3 children in those years of the 1950's. During this time, he developed a great love for acting and thanks to his mother, he studied dramatic arts with Mr. Telly Savalas before he became an actor in 1959. He went to Puerto Rico and like it very much eventually his mother move down there with his sister his older brother stay back in New York City at mulberry St. His Spanish was a disaster and he drop out of school and when to work to help his mother.

He was called to the army for the Vietnam war but never saw action; he returned to Puerto Rico. After his discharge, he entered the University of Puerto Rico his Spanish was better by now, he did drop out, returned to New York City to Mulberry St, and moved in with his father and his family for a while.

He started to work at the bankers' trust bank, but he decided to return to Puerto Rico. He was needed back home. He entered the Insurance Industry as a salesman and stayed in it.

He got this idea to write by just going back to past and remembering many things that happened in those years and looking at the present; he is set in trying a go at it. The first step is the big one and he has confidence he can pull it off. He is very sorry his mother is not alive to see it.